Dear Parents and Educators,

Welcome to Penguin Young Readers! As parents and educators, you know that each child develops at his or her own pace—in terms of speech, critical thinking, and, of course, reading. Penguin Young Readers recognizes this fact. As a result, each Penguin Young Readers book is assigned a traditional easy-to-read level (1–4) as well as a Guided Reading Level (A–P). Both of these systems will help you choose the right book for your child. Please refer to the back of each book for specific leveling information. Penguin Young Readers features esteemed authors and illustrators, stories about favorite characters, fascinating nonfiction, and more!

Corduroy's Hike

LEVEL **3**

GUIDED
READING
LEVEL **J**

This book is perfect for a **Transitional Reader** who:
• can read multisyllable and compound words;
• can read words with prefixes and suffixes;
• is able to identify story elements (beginning, middle, end, plot, setting, characters, problem, solution); and
• can understand different points of view.

Here are some **activities** you can do during and after reading this book:
• Setting: The setting of the story is where it takes place. Discuss the setting or settings of this story. Use some evidence from the text to describe the setting(s).
• Story Map: A story map is a visual organizer that helps explain what happens in a story. On a separate piece of paper, create a story map of this story. The map should include the beginning (who are the characters and what will they be doing?), the middle (what are the characters doing after the story gets started?), and the ending (how does the story end?).

Remember, sharing the love of reading with a child is the best gift you can give!

—Sarah Fabiny, Editorial Director
  Penguin Young Readers program

*Penguin Young Readers are leveled by independent reviewers applying the standards developed by Irene Fountas and Gay Su Pinnell in *Matching Books to Readers: Using Leveled Books in Guided Reading,* Heinemann, 1999.

PENGUIN YOUNG READERS
An Imprint of Penguin Random House LLC

Penguin supports copyright. Copyright fuels creativity, encourages diverse voices,
promotes free speech, and creates a vibrant culture. Thank you for buying an authorized edition
of this book and for complying with copyright laws by not reproducing, scanning, or distributing any
part of it in any form without permission. You are supporting writers and allowing Penguin to
continue to publish books for every reader.

Copyright © 2001 by Penguin Random House LLC. All rights reserved. First published in 2001 by
Viking Children's Books. This edition published in 2019 by Penguin Young Readers, an imprint of
Penguin Random House LLC, 345 Hudson Street, New York, New York 10014. Manufactured in China.

The Library of Congress has catalogued the Viking edition
under the following Control Number: 2001000509

ISBN 9781524790868 (pbk)   10 9 8 7 6 5 4 3 2 1
ISBN 9781524790875 (hc)   10 9 8 7 6 5 4 3 2 1

CORDUROY'S Hike

by Alison Inches
illustrated by Allan Eitzen
based on the characters created by Don Freeman

Penguin Young Readers
An Imprint of Penguin Random House

Lisa checked her backpack.

Peanut butter sandwich.

Juice. Hat. Jacket.

"You have to stay here, Corduroy,"

Lisa said.

"You might get lost on a hike."

I will not get lost, thought Corduroy.

He crawled into the backpack.

I will be safe in here.

Beep! Beep! The bus had come.

Lisa sat next to Susan.

"What did you bring?" asked Susan.

Lisa opened her backpack.

"A peanut butter sandwich.

Juice. And *Corduroy!*

How did you get in here?

You might get lost on a hike."

"He will be safe in your backpack,"

said Susan.

Lisa hoped Susan was right.

At the park,

Lisa and Susan found a stream

with a bridge over it.

They dropped sticks into the water.

Then they ran across the bridge.

The sticks came out the other side.

"I see mine!" they cried.

Then it was time to hike.

Off they went.

Bounce! Bounce! Bounce!

Corduroy bounced along

in the backpack.

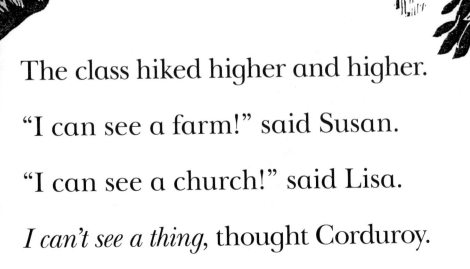

The class hiked higher and higher.

"I can see a farm!" said Susan.

"I can see a church!" said Lisa.

I can't see a thing, thought Corduroy.

Corduroy poked his head out.

That's better, thought Corduroy.

Now I can see, too.

Bounce! Bounce! Bounce!

Corduroy bounced along

in the backpack.

This is fun, thought Corduroy.

Look, no hands!

Whoops!

Corduroy bounced out
of the backpack . . .

Thud!

. . . and onto the trail.

Lisa will pick me up, he thought.

But Lisa did not pick him up.

Lisa will come back for me.

But Lisa did not come back.

Soon two hikers came by.

They picked up Corduroy.

"You must have an owner,"

said one hiker.

She set Corduroy on a branch.

"Your owner will see you

up here," she said.

Corduroy waited for Lisa.

He sang songs.

He watched the birds.

Then he saw a Cub Scout troop

hiking up the trail.

"Look!" said a Cub Scout. "A bear!"

The Cub Scout picked up Corduroy

and tossed him in the air.

Then he tossed him to another boy.

They tossed Corduroy

back and forth.

Corduroy felt like a football.

Another boy ran ahead.

Corduroy flew through the air.

They did it again.

And again.

And again.

Then, *thud!*

Corduroy landed on

the side of the trail.

The Cub Scouts walked on.

20

Corduroy tried to stand up.

He felt dizzy.

He tipped to one side.

He tipped to the other.

Then Corduroy tipped over.

Splash!

Oh my! thought Corduroy.

The water took Corduroy away.

It took him over rocks

and under a bridge . . .

Then, *zoom!*

Corduroy zoomed over a waterfall.

25

He zoomed under another bridge.

Bonk!

He stopped on a rock.

Oh dear, thought Corduroy.

I think I am stuck.

And I am cold.

And wet.

And more lost.

Soon it began to get dark.

The class came back

down the trail.

Lisa sat down.

Corduroy was gone.

She had looked everywhere for him.

The teacher clapped her hands.

"Time to get on the bus!"

Lisa sat next to the window.

Susan sat beside her.

"I was playing the stick

game again," she said.

"My sticks all came out

on the other side."

Lisa nodded.

"Something else came out
on the other side, too," said Susan.

"Corduroy!" cried Lisa.

"I'm so glad I've got you."

Me too, thought Corduroy.